FROM JAPAN WITH LOVE BEYOND TIME

A Novelette

George Baffour

DEDICATION

To the dreamers...

To those who believe in every human being's right to love, life, liberty and the pursuit of happiness, regardless of race, gender, sexual orientation or religion;

To the visionaries who are shaping the way we think as a species;

And to those who believe in the potential of technology to lift mankind into a higher plane of existence.

To the dreamers...

ACKNOWLEDGMENTS

With thanks to my greatest fan—my mother.

PROLOGUE

As I stepped off the large Boeing 777-300ER and onto the passenger ramp, it was incredibly obvious that something was terribly wrong. Oddly, we were not parked at a jetway bridge outside the international terminal of San Francisco International Airport. Rather, All Nippon Airways Flight 008 was confined within a gigantic hangar which was likely one of SFO's secluded hangars, far from the terminals.

Pausing on the ramp, I glanced to my right at the plane's enormous right wing, gazed up at the extensive ceiling far above me and then lowered my eyes to the multitude of rather strange-looking military vehicles on the tarmac below, interspersed with ambulances and over ten black buses surrounding the aircraft. I couldn't believe what I was seeing. *What on Earth was going on?*

Also upon the ramp were the Captain and Cabin Supervisor, who stood protectively to my left, just outside the aircraft door. I glimpsed at them inquiringly, but there wasn't much time to take stock of the situation now, for before me—at the summit of the stairs—were three armed military personnel, clad in hazmat suits. "Ma'am, could you kindly descend the stairs to the personnel below?" instructed one.

"What's going on?"

"Ma'am, please disembark and everything will be explained to you shortly."

"But I don't—"

Another soldier shouted, "Ma'am there's no time for this. We need everyone off the plane, NOW!"

I quickly moved for the stairs just as another frantic passenger bumped into me from behind. Down the staircase I went and into a waiting crowd of ten soldiers, also in hazmat suits. One of them—a lady—patted me down while another scanned me with a Geiger counter. I was then led to a table where I was instructed to dump my phone, watch and all other belongings into an open plastic box. While taking off my beloved yellow gold *Panthère de Cartier*, I quickly noted the time—it was 9:25 a.m.

I handed the female soldier my watch and she glanced at it with approval. "Classic," she said, as she nodded in admiration, before placing it gently into the

1

large box with my handbag and the rest of my belongings. She also received my smartphone and Kindle Fire. "Seat number, Ma'am?"

"14C."

The soldier nodded and ticked off something on her clipboard. "Dr. Melissa Dawn?" I realized that this little operation was certainly not a joke. They already had the passenger manifest and knew exactly what they were doing. Surely, they must have been ready for us several hours before our arrival.

"Yes."

"Thank you, Ma'am, and sorry for the inconvenience. A necessary evil, I'm afraid. Everything will be explained in due time." I was then escorted to the first of the buses scattered about the airplane.

Climbing aboard, I claimed a right window seat towards the middle row of the vehicle, followed closely by other passengers. I peered around and noticed that all the windows were blacked out and the driver compartment was sealed off from the passenger compartment.

Settling into my seat, I observed the boarding passengers and caught sight of Adrian. Also flying Business Class, he had sat in Seat 7A, which was a window seat on the left side of the plane, seven rows in front of mine. Dr. Adrian D'Alessandro was a dynamic 39-year-old Greek and an entrepreneur who now called San Fran' his home. His latest project was a nanotechnology startup called Sandro Nanotech, which he claimed was in *stealth mode*, whatever that meant. He held a PhD in Condensed Matter Physics from the University of Oxford and had friends in very high places ranging from Airbus SE to the UK Ministry of Defense, and he was always on the odd trip to some place or the other.

Sometimes he would tell me where he had been and what he was doing, yet sometimes he'd quip, "If I had to tell you that, I'd have to kill you." More than once, I was almost certain this was true. He was an old friend and it was only when I boarded ANA Flight 008 back in Japan that I had realized we were on the same plane. Now, as he walked down the aisle of the bus, I reached out, grabbed his hand and asked, "Adrian, what's going on?"

He paused, looked at me through his very calm, intelligent eyes and gave my hand a quick squeeze. "I don't know. I'm sure it must be a terrorist threat. Maybe there was a bomb or something aboard. But relax, we are safe now. This should be over soon." He was always so composed and was rarely ruffled by anything. He moved just a little further down the aisle and claimed the window seat right behind me.

Once our bus was full, the vehicle immediately revved to life and we began moving. Knowing California so well, and being that the military had jurisdiction over us, it was obvious to me where we were now headed. Travis Air Force Base in Solano County was the major air force base closest to SFO.

I turned around and peered at Adrian over my headrest. "Travis'?"

My smart friend nodded in agreement. "Almost certainly."

I slumped back in my seat and wondered where John must be right now. I could almost see him being frantic at the arrival hall of SFO's International Terminal, awaiting my return.

CHAPTER ONE

John Carlyle and I first bumped into each other in the high desert of Mohave, California, at the Ansari XPRIZE showdown of Wednesday, the twenty-ninth of September 2004. Only twenty-five years old, he was a young but successful marketing manager at the 3M Company in Minnesota, while I was a brilliant nineteen-year-old finishing my bachelors in psychology at Yale University.

He gawked when he noticed me for the first time. He strutted over without inhibition and uttered his first words to me ever, "You are *absolutely* stunning! Do you know how rare it is for a redhead to have light blue eyes like yours?"

I smiled shyly. "Tell me about it. It's my blessing and it's my curse."

That was it. Once we started talking that day, we found that we couldn't stop. I soon revealed to him that my dream was to be the first psychologist on man's maiden Martian settlement. His wild blue eyes, as raging as my sister's, narrowed as he chuckled and then he called me *weird*. He immediately proceeded to confess how *he also* had always wanted to go to Mars. I reciprocated by also calling him weird. So, there we were, two *weird* people, a perfect match made in the cosmos.

Seeing the privately-developed SpaceShipOne detach from the underbelly of its carrier airplane—the White Knight—and shoot off into space for the first time triggered a special kind of excitement in us. After witnessing the dawn of a new age in spaceflight, romance was inevitable. Our ensuing passionate but brief affair blazed throughout the competition and ended soon after SpaceShipOne won the Ansari XPRIZE by successfully carrying out its second trip to space on the morning of Monday, the fourth of October. Our two lives in Minnesota and New Haven were worlds apart.

It was eleven years and several failed relationships later that I bumped into him again, this time in New York, at the awards ceremony of the Wendy Schmidt Ocean

Health XPRIZE, on the evening of Monday, the twentieth of July 2015. He was now a thirty-six-year-old PhD and marketing lead at Chemours, a new Delaware-based company spun off from DuPont's performance chemicals business, while I was thirty and a full psychology professor on tenure at the University of Tokyo. He had been single for three years while I had been for two, and we both had no kids. The passionate affair of 2004 resumed in full force but this time, having nothing to lose, we decided to have a go at a real relationship.

Loving each other while living on different continents was such sweet pain. The days spent away from him were difficult, while the times spent together both in Delaware and Japan were the happiest and most fulfilling days of my life. Apart, we would lose ourselves in our regular WhatsApp communication, and together, we would lose ourselves *in ourselves* as we basked in the throes of constant lovemaking and sweet conversations that lingered forever in our own timeless love wonderland.

After two years, it was inevitable that someone would want more. John proposed in May 2017 while on a five-day surprise trip to visit me in Japan. I said yes before the weekend and after the weekend, I said no, just prior to his departure. I was scared. I felt this would destroy the miracle we both shared, and that outdooring our coupling would kill the uncompromising need we had for each other. I got us into pointless talk about how I couldn't fathom a formal long-distance marriage. *What about kids? What about family?* I could not see how two power-packed professionals could grow a family while apart, and yet keep the love. After he left, I immediately regretted my answer.

The following four weeks were the most lonesome and lost days of my life. He was the only lover I had ever felt was not going to negatively impact the direction of my life nor my dreams in any way. He had never demanded anything that would hold back my ambitions and he desired me, despite my age and my unpreparedness for kids heretofore. Regardless of our imperfect situation, he was my perfect fit. We understood each other.

The longing turned to tears, the tears turned to desperation, and the desperation finally turned to reason and resolution. At 12:40 p.m. on Wednesday, the twenty-eighth of June, I made a frantic call to John, who was then back in San Fran' visiting his parents. "I'm flying home today, John. I need to see you... we need to talk."

It was 8:40 p.m. back in San Francisco and from the husky sound of John's voice, I knew I had obviously woken him up from an early night's sleep. "Fine." He was cold.

"I'm booking ANA to SFO. Just pick me up, will ya?"

After the call, I picked up my smartphone, booked the 3:45 p.m. flight to San Francisco on All Nippon Airways Flight 008, and was lucky enough to secure a window seat in Business Class. *Seat 14C. Great!*

y 1:40 p.m. Uber ride to Haneda International Airport was spent daydreaming as I watched the beautiful scenes of Tokyo pass by my window. Since my mid-teens, I had always known I'd want to live here one day, at least for a few years.

My love of all things Japanese came from my dad. My father was Caucasian but, oddly enough, he had close ties with this place and spoke fluent Japanese. He had learnt the language all in *the name of work*, he told us when we were kids. While still in senior high school, he brought me to Japan for one of my summer holidays. This vacation was special to me, for this time it was only him and I. Mum had taken Jennifer to tour her college for the first time, but I had opted to follow Dad on one of his *business* trips. As I had recently been going through tough times dealing with my teenage disillusionment in finding myself, he was elated at the idea and thought it would give us some alone time to bond and talk about life.

Those four weeks in Japan with Dad were some of the best moments in my life. I had my big, strong father all to myself and he proudly showed me off to his Japanese friends. I had never seen him prouder of me. Dad was a redhead like myself and together we looked like a pair of matchsticks. Having taken so much after him, it was clear to anyone who saw us together that I was his daughter. He occasionally left me to laze in the hotel for stretches at a time when he had to go for *work-related* meetings, but most of the time we found ourselves on the town. We went everywhere and tried everything. Dad toured me through *Otowa-san Kiyomizu-dera*, an historic Buddhist temple in Kyoto dedicated to *Kannon*, the goddess of mercy; the hilltop *Himeji Castle* in Hyōgo Prefecture; the Hiroshima Peace Memorial Park; and a dozen other beautiful places. Our evenings were spent exploring the thousands of delicious food offerings Japanese culture had to offer. It was at this time that I developed a love for sushi, *soba*, *shabu-shabu* and last but not least, *ramen*, to satisfy my late-night cravings.

While we gorged ourselves with *food, glorious food* every night, Dad would take time to have us slowly thrash out my teenage issues, which were quite unique. Growing up a redhead child with rare blue eyes and lots of freckles, I had become accustomed to all the stereotypical pros and cons—both teasing and adoration—that came with the territory, at school and in town, and there wasn't a *ginger* quip on Earth that I had not heard before. I never felt bothered about being unique and grew quite comfortable in my own skin. But with the onset of puberty, things changed *very* rapidly. My sizeable boobs burst on the scene, my freckles vanished and my figure transformed into that of a goddess. All of a sudden, all the boys' teasing turned into obsessive attraction, which I hadn't been ready for. There were a few nice guys but the rest were mostly stupid ones, all fanatically preoccupied with trying to find out whether my pubic hair was also red.

Naturally, I soon found myself the hate of every girl in school, because I was a drop-dead-gorgeous anomaly who didn't strive to be the most popular *princess* in school and being Prom Queen was not my life's greatest ambition. I wanted more from life. I was constantly buried in books, documentaries on YouTube and outdoor adventures—at my senior high', this wasn't a good thing. S, the boys were after me *big time*, while most girls hated me *big time*, and the worst part was I had to simultaneously deal with my own feelings of bewilderment stemming from my need to figure out what I wanted from life.

And then came *Dad to the rescue*. Over those few weeks with my father in Japan, he helped me talk through my feelings, to acknowledge the things that truly mattered to me, and to decide to chase only dreams that were my own, not of society. He gave me strength and gave me courage to choose my own purpose. Dad also told me many stories of his own life and gave me insights into his life that I would never have fathomed before. For the first time, Dad revealed to me what he *really* did for a profession. At the end of that vacation with Dad, I didn't want to leave Japan. Now, many years later, I found myself resident in Tokyo. In a strange way, I guess I lived here as a way to feel close to him *again*, even though he was resting in peace, somewhere.

Abruptly, my thoughts returned to John. As the Uber driver took us onto Rainbow Bridge I stared down at Daiba Park, sitting comfortably amid the blue waters of Tokyo Bay. I then lifted my eyes beyond it to the entertainment district of *Odaiba*. Even from up here on Rainbow Bridge I could still make out Decks Toyko Beach, where John and I had often gone to dine and shop. I looked towards the right and took in the Odaiba Statue of Liberty. John and I had also enjoyed many cool nights in Odaiba looking at this spot, while sneaking tons of kisses and chatting the night away. So many memories. We were so good together. *What was I going to do once we met in San Fran'? What would I say?*

When we turned onto Metropolitan Expressway, my daydream drifted to the flight ahead and I smiled as I remembered one of the unique flying comforts I treasured on ANA—ANA's new planes offered women's only lavatories with bidets. I loved ANA because I *loved* good brands—I loved to associate myself with names that stood for quality and meaning. ANA had grown on me for another reason as well—I had written several articles for their inflight magazine *Wingspan*. With time, I was hooked and ANA became part of my personal brand, just like the XPRIZE, which I strived to patronize anytime I had the opportunity. If All Nippon Airways could take me where I was headed, I would be on it, and if not, then I would be sticking with another partner within Star Alliance.

"Madam, we're here!" The driver snapped me out of my musing.

"I'm sorry. I was thinking." *Incredible.* I checked the time and realized the ride had only been a swift thirty minutes. I didn't want it to end so soon.

The driver turned to me from his seat, smiled politely and bowed his head very slightly. "It is very good to think, Madam, but always remember to make your thoughts and desires come true. Just remember this Japanese Proverb, 'Time flies like an arrow'. Don't let time pass you by without claiming from life what is *yours*."

I smiled back at the wise fifty-plus-year-old Uber driver, who looked very much like *Mr. Miyage* from the movie *The Karate Kid*, and then proceeded to exit the vehicle. "*Sayōnara.*"

"*Sayōnara, Madamu.*" He waved happily and drove off, leaving me at the entrance to Haneda Airport's International Terminal.

Having only a small carry-on for this impromptu trip and having already checked in online, I had a little more time to kill before boarding commenced. I savagely murdered this time by grabbing a bite of crisp *tempura* on rice at *Ginza Ogura* restaurant, situated in the very popular *Edo Market Place*, a Japanese-themed food market on the fourth floor of the International Terminal.

It wasn't long before an announcement went out for Business Class passengers flying on ANA Flight 008. I proceeded to my boarding gate and after being welcomed aboard by the lovely cabin crew in the galley, I immediately ran into Adrian D'Alessandro—tucked into window seat 7A—just as I emerged into the Business Class cabin. "You turn up in the oddest situations, Adrian. Are we on another strange assignment again?"

He lifted his head to discover his accuser and then laughed, rather pleased to see me. "Dr. Melissa Dawn, what a surprise! Well, as you know, if I had to tell you that, I'd have to—"

"Never mind, I know the rest," I cut him off with a giggle. We chitchatted briefly before I headed to my own window seat seven rows down and settled comfortably into 14C. I had chosen 14C because I always preferred a seat nearer to the engines. This was a habit I had picked up from my sister Jennifer—a plane freak—because something about the sheer power at take-off always gave me a high. *The louder the better.*

Soon, true to form, the General Electric GE90 turbofans lived up to their reputation as the largest and most powerful engines in the world, and we lunged forward with force, taking off with Japanese punctuality at 3:45 p.m. sharp. As we banked eastwards, I took off my rather lovely Cartier, adjusted it from Japan

Standard Time to Pacific Time—11:45 p.m. PT—and settled in for what I anticipated would be a smooth 9-hour-25-minute flight.

After reaching cruising altitude, meals were served, and when darkness steadily overtook us with the setting of the sun, most passengers drifted to sleep. I hadn't expected the brief but terrible stint of turbulence that hit us while the cabin crew were serving beverages at 4:55 a.m. Pacific Time, about five hours and ten minutes into the flight. Over the course of two minutes, this turbulence grew so violent that when it stopped all very suddenly, I could see some of the cabin crew were sprawled on the floor, struggling to get up. When beverage service resumed, passengers who had previously been served found that their teas and coffees were completely cold.

From then on, the flight was all smooth sailing, thankfully. The only hint of any trouble brewing was at sunrise when the flight attendants instructed us to keep all window blinds down for the remainder of the flight, *even for landing.*

"Why?" was the question from seat 10E.

"Oh, nothing Ma'am. Captain's orders. It's dreadful weather outside and the Captain doesn't want any passengers getting alarmed."

I should have known she was lying, for the flight was too smooth and there seemed to be spurts of frantic but hushed chitchat among the cabin crew. And besides, it was standard procedure for aircraft window blinds to always be open upon take-off and landing. *What had the Captain revealed to them?* Upon our very soft landing, we were still instructed to keep our window blinds down. This was all so very peculiar, but nothing could have prepared me for what waited for us outside the plane.

Now here we were on military buses with blacked out windows, heading to what Adrian and I suspected would be Travis Air Force Base, where we would inevitably be briefed and undergo lengthy interrogations. About what? I didn't know, but this was definitely going to be a long day. We didn't even have access to our phones. *At what time today would I finally be reunited with John to tell him what I had to say?*

CHAPTER TWO

was right. We disembarked at Travis Air Force Base and were immediately ushered into an expansive auditorium where we would be briefed on what was going on. There were seats ready for us and a small podium, upon which stood two generals and one dark-suited gentleman who undoubtedly worked for the government—he seemed to be in charge of the operation. We took our seats and he broke away from the generals to get the ball rolling. Moving to the lectern, he addressed us, introducing himself as Dr. Hans Schmidt and informing us that he worked for the National Security Agency—NSA.

Hans Schmidt. I pondered over the name. I didn't know why it felt *so* familiar.

After a few more preambles, Dr. Schmidt finally moved on to explain our bizarre situation. Nothing could have prepared me for the absurdity of his next words. "It is apparent that, except for your pilots, you are all not aware that your flight went missing just over five hours after leaving Tokyo."

The crowd murmured. I was dumbfounded.

Amid the loud mumbling from the crowd, Dr. Schmidt paused in thought briefly and then proceeded to go straight to the point. "You won't believe this but though today *is* indeed the twenty-eighth of June, it is not the twenty-eighth of June 2017. This is the year 2037."

Despite the blatantly abnormal nature of our current predicament, most of my fellow passengers immediately burst into throes of laughter, thinking this to be some mild attempt at humor, but not me. I glanced over at Adrian seated to my right and he looked back at me. He wasn't laughing either. We both knew this must be the real deal.

Dr. Schmidt remained straight-faced. "I'm sorry, but this is no joke! You've all been missing for *exactly... twenty... years.*"

Once again, the throng continued to laugh, while Adrian and I remained dead serious. For a reason known mainly to me, I knew much about the NSA, and I knew what big a deal it was to assemble all 345 of us here in this hallowed location. At this point, there was nothing Dr. Schmidt could have said that I would have doubted. If he had informed us that the Looney Toons had invaded the Earth, I would have personally asked him to put a damned gun in my hand and point the way to bloody Acme Toon Town, without so much as a snigger. He certainly wasn't joking. This was the *Real McCoy*.

The subsequent couple of days were occupied with a barrage of medical tests and countless interrogations by government personnel. We were interviewed both singly and in groups, all captured on camera, and were asked the same questions repeatedly, yet our stories remained unchanged—the flight had been uneventful. No one remembered anything out of the ordinary.

Six days into our internment at Travis Air Force Base, two soldiers came to my makeshift quarters in one of the hangars and escorted me through parts of the base I had not been before, ending up at Dr. Schmidt's office. Stepping through the door, I had my first wow moment with 2037 technology. It was 3D holographic footage being beamed down from four points on the ceiling; this was undoubtedly the current state of television. CNN was showing several US Presidents greeting a man who was evidently the United Nations Secretary-General. The news ticker read, *UN Secretary-General in US for fourth of July Celebrations*. I noticed a 91-year-old—but still tall and upright—President Trump conversing with a stately 75-year-old President Obama, accompanied by a still gorgeous Michelle Obama. And what a surprise, the current US President was a woman! I listened to catch her name but Dr. Schmidt put off the holographic TV with a wave of his hand.

"Happy fourth of July, Dr. Dawn," he proclaimed from behind his desk, where he was standing to welcome me.

Golly. With all the fuss going on I had forgotten what day it was. America was 261 years old. "Thank you, Dr. Schmidt. With all the goings on, I had completely forgotten," I replied sarcastically, as I walked in. The two soldiers, still outside, shut the door behind me.

"Oh, please call me Hans," he insisted, as he beckoned me to sit on one of two high-back guest chairs opposite him. Dr. Schmidt seemed to be a polite man and was quite courteous.

I obeyed and settled into a chair. "Call me Melissa."

Being our first time truly alone, I now had a chance to look over Dr. Hans Schmidt up close and in detail. He was a tall well-built individual with jet black hair and the darkest, blackest eyes I had ever seen. It was fair to say he was a pretty awesome specimen of a man, with extraordinary handsomeness. Yet, his chiseled exterior and charmingly angelic face seemed to hold back a powerful and heavy mind that had seen some of the worst things this world had to offer. One simply didn't get into such an elevated position in his line of work without having tasted deeply of the *fruit of the tree of knowledge of good and evil*. However, I still couldn't figure out one thing—why was the name *Dr. Hans Schmidt* so awfully familiar?

"Coffee?"

"No thank you, Hans."

"Melissa," he got straight to the point, "you've all been here for six days but after our investigations, we have exactly... *zilch*."

I nodded.

"Now, it is important for you to know that we can't hold you all much longer without cause. This is *not* 2017. This is 2037 and we respect your rights."

At his words, I felt relieved. *This could all be over soon.* "I understand."

"We are happy that ANA Flight 008 survived and though we shall be keeping things on the low, we intend to release everyone to their families, unless it be in the interest of national security to retain you."

"Great." *Just get me out of here.*

He continued, "Your families will all be privately briefed but that is as far as it goes. All information about your encounter is classified and there won't be news in the press about how 345 passengers resurfaced twenty years after going missing. In order to protect you from public scrutiny while you assimilate into society, all adult passengers are being registered as long-time employees of the US Department of Defense, except several Japanese passengers who will return to Tokyo as foreign agents working for the Japanese Ministry of Defense.

"Don't worry. You have my silence."

"Oh, I'm not worried about that," he brushed off my comment and quickly returned to the theme of his exposition. "Let me be straight with you. The pilots recall nothing extraordinary except weird instrument readings which lasted only during a bout of turbulence about five hours into the flight. This bumpiness was brief but we estimate that it was at this point that some effect, some...," he searched the air for the word, "... force majeure...," he had found it, "... caused your plane to jump to this time."

I nodded, indicating my agreement with his hypothesis.

"Yet, no one remembers anything else. We need a clue that will help us figure this thing out. Now, the reason I have called you here is that you are a psychologist, and a damn good one, I dare say."

"Why, thank you Hans."

"If anyone can give us objective clues about what happened, it's you." He paused, leaned forward and continued, "And besides, your dad was with the NSA, so I know you understand the value of what we are doing here."

I bowed my head at the thought of my father. The cat was out of the bag but then again, I already expected that any man in Dr. Schmidt's capacity would easily find out about my belated father's years of dedicated service to the NSA.

"May he rest in perfect peace," he said. "He was a great man. Coincidentally, your dad also knew *my* father."

I wondered what their connection had been. "Really? Which agency was your dad in?"

"Well, it's a long story we can share over a drink one day. But yes, we *both* are kids of agency men. And that's the point I am making, that you—above all the other passengers—comprehend the national security implications of this event. You're the only witness with the professional objectivity to help us meticulously unravel what happened to Flight 008."

"I am flattered by your comments, Hans, but you know what? You never mentioned which agency you are *really* from. You're clearly not NSA like everyone else."

He shrugged it off, smiling with admiration at my sharpness. "It doesn't really matter Mel. What does matter is that I am here trying to figure this out for all our sakes. And you must know that this concerns much more than just *national* security." He rose from his desk, walked to the window behind his chair, gazed out through the blinds and took a breather.

I actually did agree with him. Whatever his agenda was, it was more than just *national*. It had *global* significance. "Okay, Hans. Let's do this."

"Great!" He was ecstatic.

"So, how can I help?"

Dr. Schmidt returned to his chair and sat. "Would you be willing to undergo hypnotic regression?" he asked, as casually as offering me tea and biscuits.

Unbelievable! This man was truly desperate—but so was I. I needed to get out and find John. "If you think it will help uncover any clues to unravel what happened, then let's get this show on the road." The sooner I could be out of here, the better.

The chaise lounge felt cozy as I drifted into hypnosis, guided by Dr. Mark Lewis, another odd character in my internment saga at Travis Air Force Base.

"Now, let's skip to the part of the flight right before the turbulence started," he asked.

13

"Okay."

"What do you see, Melissa?"

"It's been over five hours since leaving Haneda International Airport. I feel restless so I get up to stretch my legs."

"Really?"

"I have not been up this whole flight, so I decide to take a short stroll through the airplane."

"You didn't mention this before, during our earlier interrogations."

"I honestly didn't remember then, but now that I do, this all feels so strange."

"Go on, Dr. Dawn."

"I'm in Business Class walking towards First Class. Everyone is asleep except the guy in the aisle seat 8E, who is engrossed in watching *Westworld*—a great series by the way. I exit Business Class and stretch at the aircraft door by the lavatories. I notice the cabin crew are preparing for beverage service so I quickly take advantage of the free aisles to stroll back towards Economy. Most passengers are asleep, but the traveler in seat 19A notices me and coughs inquisitively as if to say *I've seen you. What are you up to?* I ignore the nosy parker and continue towards the back of the plane."

"Why are you smiling, Melissa?"

"The lady dozing in seat 26A looks ridiculously funny in her strange pose. Her mouth is wide open against the window. Now she is changing positions and adjusting her ear plugs."

"Oh, alright." Dr. Lewis patiently persisted. "Go on."

"Whoops! Beverage service is starting. I head for my seat in Business Class before the aisles get busy. But that's odd!"

"What?"

Nothing... oh my!" I shouted.

"Tell me. What's happening?"

"I see him," I whispered.

"I can't hear you, Mel. Did you say you see... him? See who?"

"Oh, my..."

"What! What do you see Dr. Dawn?"

"That's why the tea was so cold," I mumbled to myself.

"What was that, Melissa? Please speak up Dr."

I had become aware of myself and realized that I shouldn't reveal what I was seeing. "I'm trying Dr. but... I see nothing. Everyone seems so... normal. There is slight turbulence but beverage service still continues."

"Are you sure?" Dr. Lewis was on to me. I had to get smart.

"Yes, but I want to know more. I wish I could see more so we know what happened." Here came my best Hollywood impression *ever*. I pretended to cry. "But I can't... I can't see anything." I drew all the tears I could muster and put off the best *poor and perturbed damsel in distress* show I could.

Dr. Lewis slowly began to back off. "It's okay, Melissa." He had fallen for it. "You are safe now. Nothing can harm you. Let us return to real life. Come back to me."

Dr. Lewis carefully brought me out of hypnosis. I sat up, and through my waterfalls of false tears, I could see a disappointed Dr. Schmidt pacing slowly across the room.

"I'm sorry, Dr. Schmidt, but there was nothing out of the ordinary." I lied—I now remembered *every* shocking detail. *Oh, my gosh! Oh, my effing gosh!*

Back in my quarters, I sat in shock, unable to believe what had really happened on that plane. I was damned if I was going to reveal what was going on without thinking this through. If they realized what I now knew, I would not get to see John again for a very long time. I knew how these people worked. I was certainly not going to reveal the truth to Dr. Schmidt—not yet—or he'd keep me here for ages until they solved this thing. And I *so* needed to see John. I didn't care about anything else right now.

CHAPTER THREE

Having been kept from all knowledge of the outside world thus far, we the passengers of ANA Flight 008 wondered what the world of 2037 would be like. Some had grandiose visions of a Star-Trek-type world, but I knew better. It had only been twenty years and I knew technology would surely have progressed exponentially, however I felt people would still be people—lovers, haters, progressives and luddites. I suspected that at the heart of it all, families would still be the driving force behind our lives. I would soon find out if I was right.

Two soldiers escorted me out to Travis Air Force Base's reception where my family was waiting to receive me. I emerged to see my younger sister and mother beaming back at me but looking only a bit older. Jennifer's blue eyes were still vivid but her blonde hair had developed grey undertones. Mama was seventy-five years old, yet strangely, she seemed remarkably fit. They took in the sight of me looking just as I did twenty years ago. As we approached one another, I began to cry and so did they, while Jennifer's daughter—21-year-old Diana—looked on with a smile. She had been just a baby when I last saw her.

It was only after coming out of our sobs, kisses and hugs that I had the presence of mind to let my eyes stray and grab a proper look at the 2037 world. My family watched as I broke away and slowly inched toward the tall glass walls to gaze out at midday Solano County. The Californian summer sky was as blue as it had ever been. All at once, I felt home again, like I was still somehow back in 2017. We were one floor up and I could see the base's entrance with its security checkpoint, above which read, *Welcome to Travis—Gateway to the Pacific!* Looking beyond the checkpoint, I noticed a taxi pass by with neither a driver nor passenger, followed by another car with a man behind the wheel, but who was reading a newspaper as the car drove itself along. Obviously, self-driving cars had become the norm. These two cars joined other vehicles at a traffic light down the road, and when it turned green, all the vehicles launched as a single unit, as if joined together like the passenger cars of a train. *Amazing.*

My family walked up behind me and Jennifer put her right arm around me. She squeezed my shoulder and spoke in her warm and comforting tone, "There's much to catch up on, sweetie. We'll take things one step at a time. Okay?"

"Okay, sis." It felt so good to be with family again.

Jennifer drove her Tesla Model 10S to the checkpoint and exited Travis'. "Homer, plot course for home," she ordered.

Her digital assistant answered from the car's speakers, "Course plotted, Jennifer. Permission to assume control?"

"Take over. And make it the scenic route, will ya?"

The steering wheel retracted a few inches to give Jennifer more room and she let it go. We were now being driven autonomously by Homer, connected wirelessly to a centralized traffic control network. *Marvelous.* Mobility had changed so much and there was no congestion on the roads. Diana, seeing my amazement, explained how the US Traffic Control Ecosystem (USTCE) made autonomous traffic flow quickly and seamlessly.

I turned my gaze back to my family in the car and began to inspect my mother, "Mum, I can't get over how good you look. You are literally ten years younger than I left you!"

Jennifer cut in spiritedly, "Foxy Mama! You sexy *thang!*"

I continued checking her out, playfully. "But really Mama, you are so hot... so fit... so athletic, and so..."

"Firm?" was the very apt word unleashed by Jennifer. She had followed my eyes rolling up to stare at my mother's still very vivacious breasts.

"Enough! Enough of that!" Mum blurted out with a laugh, having had enough of our unbridled taunts. "It seems I raised two naughty little minxes for daughters! You haven't changed a bit Mel and I can see that Jennifer's got her *partner in comic crime* back."

"But gosh, Mama, honestly you are looking so freaking hot. What can I say?"

"Well it's the year 2037, darling," she stated with a wiggle of her neck and a snap of her fingers. "Plenty of folks are living way past 120 years now, and there's a whole range of amazing ways available to maintain your erm... your erm... your range of *equipment...* as long as you want."

"Yeah, Mel," remarked Jennifer, "and just you wait till you see her new boyfriend."

"What?" I couldn't believe it. "Boyfriend? And a *new* one at that?"

"Get off my case, baby. I have a right to have some fun."

"*Ooh la la*, Mama! Jennifer exclaimed with a chuckle. "You bad Mama Jama!"

Meanwhile, sweet Diana feigned disgust and friskily covered her ears. "I'm honestly too innocent for all this, Mum!"

And with that, Mama, Jennifer and I all jeered in sync, "*Aah*, go jump in a lake!" I felt as high as a kite. It had been twenty years since we last used this family saying together. I was exceptionally grateful for my wonderful family. We were such a strange bunch.

Mum had had only the two of us, and Jennifer took after Mum and Grandma, who had both been blonde with exceptionally dazzling blue eyes. I had *also* inherited blue eyes, but they were nowhere near as captivating as Jennifer's. As for me, I had mostly taken after Dad, with his height, fiery-red hair and passion for adventure. There were however two things that Mum, Jennifer and I had *all* inherited—and now I could tell Diana had them also—and these were Grandma's luscious breasts and her tremendously voluptuous body. It wasn't as amusing at the time, but growing up, the neighborhood had always referred to our home as the *house of hotties*.

I turned to look closer at Diana, who was a magnificent mulatto with amazing dark hair, large grey eyes and prominent dimples that would turn even the devil to mush. Her father was a brilliant Ghanaian-American scientist that Jennifer had met in college. Prior to getting in the car, Jennifer had informed me he was still working for NASA and was away for a few days on an assignment.

I decided to engage Diana in conversation and get to know her a bit better. "So why don't you tell Auntie Mel about yourself, my darling Diana? The last time I saw you, you were still in diapers."

A lovely conversation ensued and she told me of her life's ambitions and excellent academic record. I was pleased beyond words when she revealed that she was already in her fourth year at Yale. *What a genius—and at my alma mater too!*

Homer's *scenic route* took us out of Solano County and through the main areas of downtown and uptown San Francisco. The San Francisco of 2037 was a blend of the old and the new. The city's streets and buildings seemed the same from a distance, but upon closer inspection it was clear there was change everywhere. Jennifer and Mama talked me through the details.

Solar technologies had advanced so tremendously that it took a mere fraction of rooftop space to power an entire household. Still, most homeowners opted for fully solar roofs and walls—solar came in all shapes, sizes and colors—because they could feed the excess electricity into the grid and earn significant income from the power companies. US power companies used household-generated electricity to supplement supply to industries with energy shortfalls, and who often chose not to waste large expanses of empty land for their solar power generation.

Observing the city sky as we drove on, I realized one innovation that had taken off—literally—was drones. They came in many varieties and the air was full of them, though Federal Aviation Administration regulations restricted them to a low-altitude range called the *drone zone*, except when taking off or landing. The drone zone formed a dark translucent blanket over the city which—because of collision avoidance systems—moved in waves like a murmurating flock of starlings. Noticing my amazement, Jennifer explained how drones were being used for delivering all manner of things from food to online shopping, and even the morning paper—for those who still preferred traditional newspapers as a lifestyle statement. Once in a while, one would zip by on its way to delivering its cargo.

Our next waypoint was San Francisco International Airport. Jennifer, being an aerospace engineer, was excited to update me. Riding close to SFO's runways, we watched an ANA flight taking off, invariably headed back to Japan. "That's the Boeing 989 Jumbo Ray—it carries a thousand people."

"What the hell?" I was amazed at the large plane which looked like a flying stingray.

Jennifer explained how most aircraft were now built as flying wings, which allowed manufacturers to fit more of an airplane and its passengers into the same wingspan as a predecessor like the Boeing 747. These flying-wing aircraft generated substantially more lift and therefore required less power to stay airborne. However, their large surface areas created more drag at high speeds, thus they cruised in the Earth's upper atmosphere where the air was thinnest, allowing them to go hypersonic, propelled by their turbofan-scramjet engines, which ran on hydrogen. *No more hydrocarbon fuels? Yay!*

Having learned to simultaneously endure and embrace Jennifer's plane-crazy expositions as a child, I had developed quite a flair for the technical aspects of aviation, so I was genuinely absorbing every detail. "Isn't hydrogen so expensive to produce?" I asked.

"Not anymore. We figured it out." She explained how, with the improvements of solar and nuclear technologies, it had become feasible to produce hydrogen via electrolysis on a larger scale at or near the end user, thereby eliminating long and expensively complex supply chains. "Carbon-neutral aviation. Ain't it a beauty?"

All this aircraft talk reminded me of John and his love of private aviation. I wondered if he was still alive and if so, if he was still flying privately as a hobby. I was now so eager to let my sister in on the details that weren't included in her and

Mama's debriefing by Dr. Schmidt's team, but I remained quiet on the issue as I had already decided to wait till evening when the two of us would find time alone.

CHAPTER FOUR

A rriving at Jennifer's home in Haight-Ashbury, I was first at the door, which I found locked. I was dying to pee.

Jennifer caught up with me at the threshold and instructed, "Homer, add new family member."

"Certainly," his voice now emanated from a panel to the right of the door. "Level of access?"

"Full family privileges."

"Scanning iris now." I noticed a little red light flicker on the panel. "Welcome, Dr. Melissa Dawn. You now have full access privileges to this home."

Jennifer bowed dramatically with a wave of her hand, beckoning me to enter first. I moved to try the door again but it then it quickly opened on its own.

Jennifer followed with Mama. "Welcome home, sis!"

On returning from the bathroom, I headed to the living room and crashed onto Jennifer's comfortable orange leather sofa. What a relief it was to be back in a house. Learning all about the new world on the way over had gotten my brain tired. I needed to take a break.

"Don't park yourself just yet, darling," called Jennifer as she approached me. "Homer, put Amazon on screen." Instantaneously a holographic TV came on and displayed the home page for Amazon.com.

"But sis, I'm so tired." I protested.

"I know, darling," said Jennifer with a smile, "but you don't have clothes. All your stuff is archaic, and I won't have my sister looking haggard."

"Well, alright." I guessed she was right. "I *am* a little outdated, aren't I?"

"Come on, sit up. We'll shop together, like old times." Jennifer plonked herself next to me on the sofa.

Jennifer helped me pick out a few sets of clothes, bras and panties to last me a couple of days. "Now, for your makeup and Google Aug-Life."

"Aug what?" I inquired quizzically. "What the hell is that?"

"Oops! I forgot to tell you about that! It's *so important*." She was getting excited again. "They're special contact lenses from Google for living an augmented reality lifestyle. They're all the rave nowadays."

"Show me." I was damned curious now.

Jennifer then instructed Homer, "Homer, show Melissa on screen what I see with my Google Aug-Life."

Unbelievable. The TV displayed what Jennifer was seeing, except there was virtual content everywhere. *This was AR on steroids.* She turned and I saw myself on the TV with labels all over me—my name, temperature, age, date of birth, and my relationship to her. Suddenly, a blinking envelope appeared in the upper right corner, indicating she had just received a new email. Through her Google Aug-Life, Jennifer could also see Homer's avatar standing by me. He was a 6-foot man in his thirties and had slick black hair which was held in a ponytail. He wore a gray suit and looked like a young Orlando Bloom.

"And guess what?" Jennifer quizzed me. "You can also use them to surf the web, navigating a virtual screen with your mind."

"Marvelous!" I was completely hooked. "But... *with your mind?*"

"Yes, sweetheart, *with your mind*," she emphasized. "Don't worry, it's rather easy. You'll try it when you get yours."

In a few moments, Homer announced the arrival of our shopping.

Jennifer and I went to the front door and opened it to find a drone hovering before us. Jennifer checked the shopping bags on the floor, opened them, turned to the drone and said, "Okay," after which it flew away.

Back inside and seated again on the orange sofa, I unwrapped my Google Aug-Life, put the lenses on and proceeded to explore my new world when Mum walked over, clutching my new clothes. I could see every detail about her body's vitals as well as her maiden name and age.

"Mama, why didn't Homer announce another drone was here? I'd have gone to pick the bags myself."

"No darling. What you purchased were the designs. The clothes were printed in the den upstairs."

"Of course!" I had forgotten about 3D Printing.

All this change was getting overwhelming, yet I craved more. I resolved to spend the rest of the day surfing the web on my Aug-Life to catch up on as much as possible.

ours later, Jennifer found me still at it. "Sis, isn't it enough for one day? You even skipped dinner."

I smiled guiltily.

She smiled back and I continued my trip down the Rabbit Hole.

Fantastic! I was astonished at how humanity had changed. With the monumental advances in artificial intelligence, robotics, nanotechnology and 3D printing, the world's economy had turned upside down. Most mining and manufacturing jobs had gradually been replaced by tech. This trend had created a paradigm of unprecedented unemployment in the mid-2020s. Yet, renowned economists and key politicians embraced this change, realizing that this shift could be harnessed to move humanity into a higher, more dignified existence. Thus, something ingenious was crafted.

In 2028, the government instituted Universal Basic Income (UBI) for all Americans, easily funded by taxing the exponential profits arising from tech. Early critics had initially alleged that UBI would make people lazy and result in worsening the crisis, but pilot studies then proved that when people were freed from worrying about their basic needs, they tended to be liberated to pursue entrepreneurial ventures. These findings mirrored those of several other countries including Finland, the Netherlands and Sweden, who had all tried and tested the concept a decade earlier. US trials of UBI proved that in effect, humans without basic financial headaches would always be busy pursuing ideas and preoccupations that they had passion for. By 2030, this unforeseen positive consequence of UBI triggered a radical increase in startup businesses on an unprecedented scale and ultimately resulted in a massive shift of the American workforce into more white-collar entrepreneurial startups, which in turn continued to create new tech-based innovations and services, *which also in turn*, employed more people.

Apart from UBI and regular employment, another major way people made income was through the sharing economy, a multibillion-dollar industry. The advanced incorporation of blockchain technologies into managing transient ownership rights allowed more rapid sharing of goods and services as simple as toys, to things as complicated as private jets and recreational rides into space. This created an ecosystem where unused possessions were instantly utilized by those with a demand for them. Sharing had become the main social revolution of the future. Evolving through Uber, Airbnb, JustPark and other apps of the pre-2020s, a whole generation of kids had grown up with the willingness to share. This resulted in a circular economy in which all items changed ownership rapidly, on a need basis. If one man's poison was another man's meat, then that man was going to come and get it. Nothing was wasted. The world's economies became leaner and more efficient as accumulation and hording became things of the past. Individual incomes generated seamlessly through sharing were substantial and the more one shared, the wealthier one became.

As predicted by futurists of the 2010s, computing power had exploded and cloud computing was all-pervasive. Storage on personalized electronic devices became obsolete, evolving them into disposable public commodities which, when held, instantaneously accessed a user's online data, but became empty shells when not in use. Also, the omnipresence of ubiquitous computing meant that people could move freely and instantaneously access their data on-the-go through screens on walls, tables and everywhere. Yet, even this was being disrupted by the Internet of Things and the advent of the augmented reality lifestyle promised by Google's Aug-Life lenses. The impact of technology on the ease of commerce was also phenomenal. Shoppers could walk into stores, pick up items and just walk out without a word, because iris-scanning technology and IoT made checkouts become automatic unseen operations in the cloud.

My, oh my! What a world!

was lying awake in my pajamas when Jennifer entered the guest room around midnight and announced, "Everyone's in bed. I guess it's our time now, right?"

It was time to tell her the more intricate details of the whole story. "I don't know where to start, but first, I've been dying to know what happened to John. Is he alive and what happened after I vanished?"

Jenny became somber and gave a sigh.

"No, love! Don't tell me he's dead."

"Oh no! Nothing like that."

"Thank heavens." I was relieved.

"John didn't take it too well when your plane went missing. None of us did." She continued, "We kept in touch regularly while the search effort lingered on but after your trail turned cold, our calls dwindled. He got married years later and had a daughter."

My unfairly-jealous heart sank. "That's okay. Well, at least he is happy, right?"

She hesitated before giving me the bad news, "Unfortunately, no. His wife died three years ago. He then quit his job in Delaware and moved to New Mexico to take up farming on a large swath of real-estate he had inherited. His daughter is in Yale now, so he lives alone, running his high-tech farm. He is quite the wealthy recluse."

"Now, that's very sad."

"Yes, it is, isn't it?"

I now took Jennifer's hand, looked straight into her eyes and asked her what I had waited all day to. "You have to take me to him, Jenny—tomorrow. Can you do that for me?"

"What? That's so soon, Melissa."

I spoke slowly, "Jennifer, you *must* take me to him. I need to see him at least one more time, *and then* you have to take me back to Travis Air Force Base."

"Travis'! Mel, what's all this that you are suddenly going on about?"

I squeezed her hand. "Let me tell you everything." And so, I did. I told her why I was flying back to the USA from Japan twenty years ago and gave my version of how we ended up here. Finally, I told her about the hypnosis and what I remembered had actually happened on that airplane.

On hearing the frightening details of what I had come to remember, Jennifer covered her mouth as her jaw dropped in surprise. "You have to go back to Travis'! You have to tell them!"

"Exactly! *I know that,* but first I *must* see John and tell him what I left Japan to say. Will you do this for me, sis?"

"Yes."

ater that evening, I lay down reminiscing about what a day it had been. My thoughts then drifted to John and I wondered how he must be now. *Had he changed? Was he the same old strong but funny John?*

Finally, sleep came knocking at my door and I spoke out, "Homer, dim the lights please."

"Yes Ma'am." He began to dim the lights. "Say when."

"Dimmer... dimmer... dimmer... perfect."

"Save under sleep settings?"

"Yes, please."

"Your sleep preferences have been saved."

"Goodnight, Homer."

"Sleep tight, Ma'am."

I was really getting the hang of this AI digital assistant *thingamajig.*

CHAPTER FIVE

I t was like the scene out of a movie as Jennifer and I disembarked outside the main house at Carlyle Farm in New Mexico. We arrived to find John standing outside in the waning golden light of the late afternoon sun, configuring three drones to inspect the crop. Jennifer stood by the car as I slowly inched towards the house.

John lifted his eyes to inspect his visitors, dropped his control console and began to approach us. "No, it's impossible." He was squinting as he sped over, trying to be sure he was making me out correctly.

I took off my hat and unfurled my ruby-red hair, which began to blow in the breeze.

"It *is* you!" He could see I hadn't aged a bit.

I rushed forward to meet him and hugged him tighter than I ever had. "I missed you!"

"But how is this possible?" He was flabbergasted.

"It doesn't matter. What matters is that I told you we needed to meet and talk. Here I am, even though I'm twenty years late."

Jennifer looked on, herself in tears at witnessing such a moving reunion.

After a few more moments of holding each other, John and I finally released our embrace, and stepped back. He stared at me for what seemed an eternity, taking in my features all over again, and then asked the inevitable. "So... what did you want to tell me?"

Immediately my mind went back to our last goodbye twenty years ago when I had turned down his marriage proposal at Haneda International Airport, just prior to his departure back home. I remembered the torturous days that ensued and the regret I had felt—my stark helplessness at the daunting thought of ever having to live without him.

As I began to sob again, my thoughts then flew to the mysterious Uber driver who had driven me to Haneda International Airport for *my* own flight back to the States, and I recounted the enigmatic strangeness of the encounter as he had revealed the words of the Japanese proverb, "'Time flies like an arrow'. Don't let time pass you by without claiming from life what is *yours.*"

I finally understood, now more than ever, the true significance of those words. Time *did indeed* fly like an arrow. Now, with the bounds of time having fallen away, all my earlier fears and apprehensions ceased to exist. In the grand scheme of things, with time all gone, my trepidations meant nothing. Time had pulled back the curtains of anxiety and impossibility. All that remained was the true and pure love that I could not let go of.

"Baby, are you okay?" John asked again. "What did you want to tell me? I'm here *now.*"

I snapped out of my reverie and answered. "'I wanted to let you know that I've changed my mind." I couldn't stop crying. "This thing we have is the only thing that feels so right."

"My baby." He was moved and felt relieved that I still cared so much.

"I made a big mistake. What matters is this thing we have shared. If being together is what fulfills us, then surely everything else be figured out *somehow.*"

John reached for my hands and held them tight as he listened.

"Ask again. Propose again."

And so, he did. Down on one knee, he requested once more, "Dr. Melissa Dawn, you've stood me up for twenty damned years. Will you *finally marry me?*"

"Yes, and I mean it this time." At last, I had fulfilled what I set off from Japan to do twenty years ago.

Jennifer looked on, an inconsolable mess as wet makeup streamed down her face from all her tears of joy. John and I chuckled amidst our tears, went over to her, and all three of us huddled in a giant hug.

"Congratulations," said Jennifer to John, the two of them looking like siblings, with their blond heads and radiant blue eyes.

"But, farming?" I asked John.

"Go figure," he shrugged. "It's weird right: John the farmer? But it's still not as weird as you showing up after all these years with no visible signs of aging, when you're supposed to be missing on an airplane. Now *that* is weird."

"Well, trust me, things are about to get a bit weirder." I then explained to him what had happened—*everything*—and I also revealed why I had to go back to Dr. Schmidt.

He was awestruck. "Heck, Mel! Yes, you *do have to go back* to Travis'. It's real important, but know what? I'm coming along!"

"But John—"

"Look! I spent twenty years without you. If you think I'm letting you out of my sight for a moment, you're wrong. If you have to tarry at Travis', then I'm gonna be right there *witcha*."

I honestly didn't want to dissuade him and thankfully he was so insistent that he was not going to hear any more of it. "Oh, John." I was pleased.

"We must make one quick stop in town, though. There's something I gotta do."

"Sure, where are we going?"

He ignored my question. "Let me grab a fresh shirt and we'll be off."

John emerged two minutes later, talking into his Google LifeWrist, a complementary device to Google's Aug-Life contact lenses. "Hi Aussie. 'Remember that thing you did in a hurry last summer and for which you needed my help?'

I beamed, realizing who he was talking to. That was Bob, John's lifelong best friend who was originally from Perth in Australia. Everyone just called him Aussie Bob or Aussie for short. He was one of the funniest men I had ever met in my entire life.

John continued his call, "Yeah, bro. I'm going to need your help for the exact same thing in exactly thirty minutes."

"Bloody Hell!" Aussie's answer was so loud I could hear it from John's Bluetooth earpiece.

John yanked out the earpiece and barked back at Aussie, "Gee, you damned near took my ear out with that holler." He replaced the earpiece back in his right ear. "Anyway, meet me in thirty minutes, will ya? You know the deal and you know the place. See you soon." John dropped his call.

"Aussie will go crazy when he sees me. By the way, what do you need him to do for you?" I asked, while Jennifer and I started heading back to her vehicle.

John noticed us moving out to the car and called out. "No, no, no, girls. We're not going in that."

"Oh okay. Are we going in your car, then?" asked Jennifer.

"Car? No. We're going in this!" He lifted his right hand, spoke into his LifeWrist and then the large garage door behind him lifted to reveal a sleek sedan-sized aircraft of some sort. The craft was essentially an egg-shaped cabin with three ducted fans, two at the sides and one at the rear.

"Oh my gosh!" remarked Jennifer. "It sure beats the hell outta mine."

John scoffed playfully. "This is the latest creation of Burt Rutan."

I cut in. "You're frigging kidding me!" I couldn't believe it. "Burt Rutan is still alive and kicking?"

"Yup—the marvels of 2037 healthcare. He's ninety-four years old, and still trying to push the aviation envelope."

"Damn! This is one fine piece of machine, I must say." Jennifer continued to lust over the curvaceous and silvery flying capsule.

"What the heck are y'all waiting for? Hop in. It's a four-seater, we'll all fit comfortably."

"What about Jennifer's car?" I blurted, before I remembered with embarrassment that I was no longer in 2017.

"Easy," Jennifer replied casually. "I guess, I'll let it pick me up in town when we are done with our little stopover."

"Self-driving cars, Melissa," remarked John in jest, "remember those? You just drove over in one." He was enjoying teasing me.

Seizing the opportunity, Jennifer and I both rebuffed in unison, "Aah, go jump in a lake!"

CHAPTER SIX

D r. Hans Schmidt was puzzled as he walked into Travis's reception, shadowed closely by a younger dark-suited gentleman who seemed to be his aide. "Well, I certainly wasn't expecting you back here so soon, Dr. Dawn. You just left yesterday."

"The name is now Dr. *Carlyle*." I corrected him with glee and showed off my beautiful wedding ring, barely one-hour-old.

He noticed John at my side and grinned back at me in surprise. "Wow! That's fast work, Mel. Congratulations."

"Thank you, Hans," I answered politely. "And may I introduce my husband, Dr. John Carlyle?"

He stretched his hand to shake John's hand. "Pleased to meet you, Dr. Carlyle. You must be quite a guy."

John looked at Dr. Schmidt quizzically and stated very slowly, "Wait... I know you..."

Hans, looking somewhat shaken, seemed to remember something but nevertheless insisted, "Oh, I get that a lot Dr. Carlyle. I have that kind of face—I look familiar to everyone."

Still, John was very persistent, trying to put a finger on it. "No way, Dr., we *have met* before."

Dr. Schmidt tried to defer the issue by being funny, "Come on, Johnnie Boy, we can't have met before because I rarely go out of this place. My work on this base is my prison. Our paths haven't crossed." Hans looked very nervous and wanted to drop the topic quickly.

Just then, upon hearing the words *Johnnie Boy*, John seemed to finally identify Hans. "Oh yes, I remember you now. You've just gotten rid of your beard and mustache." said John with a stern look of distrust. "DHS!"

Upon hearing that hallowed acronym, Hans immediately recomposed himself, realizing it was futile to refute John's allegations. John had precisely made him out.

"So that's your real name, DHS? Dr. Hans Schmidt?" John reached out his hand to Hans and shook it again, rather mockingly. "Well, it's awfully nice to be *properly* introduced, *Dr.... Hans... Schmidt.*"

Dr. Schmidt was back to his old calm self now. "Well—charmed to see you, Johnnie—*again.*" He gave John a discreet wink, but I caught it.

"Wait a minute," I barged into the conversation. "What are you two talking about?"

"Why don't we ask the doctor here?" replied John, still looking accusingly at Hans and directing his next comment to him. "I'm sure this constitutes a *need-to-know* situation, wouldn't you think, DHS?"

Hans, unperturbed, nodded with a cool smirk and addressed me, "Why don't we discuss this later on. Right now, I want to know to what I owe the pleasure of your sudden return."

"We need to talk, Hans, I have something important to tell you."

"What's going on?"

"Hans, I lied," I blurted. "I remembered something extraordinary during the hypnosis."

"But why didn't you tell me?"

"I had to set my own affairs in order first."

"But this is a matter of national security. Surely it takes precedence over anything else."

I reached out and held the right hand of John, who stood rather protectively to my left, and I looked deep into his eyes while replying Dr. Schmidt. "No Hans, it doesn't. I have one life to live."

Hans knew he couldn't win this one, so he kept quiet.

"And besides, who knows what tomorrow brings, right"

He agreed. "Well, you're right about that, Mel. Who knows what tomorrow brings? Another twenty-year-jump, perhaps?" He smirked again.

Dr. Schmidt, followed by his aide, politely led me to the door leading from the reception to the deeper recesses of the base. He opened it and after I had entered, he remained at the entrance and turned back to John, who was still planted like a statute on our previous spot. Judging from Hans' gaze, it was obvious that John commanded some authority and mutual respect in his eyes. "You better get your ass in here, Johnnie Boy," he beckoned with a creepy grin. "Since I'm sure she's already told you what I'm about to hear, I might as well utilize your brains, *once again*, just like old times."

As John walked sternly towards the door, Hans turned to his aide and instructed, "Get the paperwork done ASAP," referring to John. He then turned to John, who had reached the door, and gave him a pat on the back as he stepped through it. "Your security clearance just went up again—by just one notch."

I caught that. John already had security clearance? What was it that John hadn't told me all these years? What level of clearance did he have previously that now he only needed one more notch to have full access to this part of the base and the investigations being carried out on ANA Flight 008?

n five minutes, we were all settled in the office of Dr. Mark Lewis and I was once again sprawled across his cozy chaise lounge, being guided into hypnosis.

Soon I was back again at the part of the flight where all the trouble started.

"There was terrible turbulence, lots of it. It was so bad that people started to scream for dear life. Returning from my walk down in Economy, I managed to make it back to my seat in Business Class and opened my window blind. I peered into the night outside and saw a green mist and balls of light darting to and fro about the plane."

John and Dr. Schmidt listened very attentively.

"Then, just as suddenly as it had started, the turbulence subsided but when I looked around, everybody was unconscious... *except me.* Even the cabin crew were lying on the floor. Suddenly, a blue beam shone through the fuselage and into the Business Class cabin."

Dr. Lewis immediately glanced over at Dr. Schmidt and Hans stared back at him knowingly, non-verbally acknowledging some knowledge they both shared and that was awoken by what they had just heard.

Dr. Lewis returned his attention to me and continued. "What did you see?"

"I couldn't believe what I was seeing."

"What is it, Mel?" Dr. Lewis was eager to hear the rest.

"A strange figure floated down the light beam into the cabin and stood in the aisle before me. It was a huge man, about seven feet tall and Scandinavian-looking, with abnormally big blue eyes and long blond hair."

This time, Dr. Lewis directed his loud stare at John, who then peered over at Dr. Schmidt, silently admitting to knowledge *he himself* also shared with Hans. "Go on, Mel."

"He was muscular and wore unusual skin-tight clothing. I tried to speak but somehow couldn't make a noise. He walked down to my seat, smiled down at me and said he needed my help." I was getting emotional now and started crying. "Soon, he stopped moving his lips but I could still hear him speak directly into my mind. He said he needed me to deliver a message for him." I was bawling now. "I'm sorry. This is overwhelming anytime I think of it."

"You're safe, Mel. Be calm. Just tell us what you saw."

"I'll try." Still deep in hypnosis and with my eyes closed, I took a breath and composed myself before continuing. "He said I'd meet one Dr. Hans Schmidt, and to give him a message."

"What!" exclaimed Hans as he stood up with a jolt. "What on Earth? He mentioned my name?" Dr. Lewis quickly waved his hand at Dr. Schmidt and signaled him to hold his fire and sit down.

"Yes, he mentioned you by name. After telling me his message, I blacked out. When I came to, I couldn't remember the encounter. Everyone else was behaving normally and going about their usual business. Being oblivious to what had just happened to me, I found it rather odd to notice the cabin crew getting up from the floor and proceeding to serve beverages. By this time, they were also very puzzled because the hot drinks had gone completely cold. Who knows how long we were all knocked out? There was still a trace of minor turbulence and green mist outside my window, which both subsided as beverage service continued."

Dr. Mark Lewis sat back in his chair, finally relieved have some decent knowledge of what had transpired on ANA Flight 008. He looked over at Dr. Schmidt and noticed him gesturing for the last pertinent question to be asked. Dr. Lewis quickly obliged him and asked me, "What was the message, Melissa?"

At last, I took a breath and then revealed everything I had been instructed to say. I had finally delivered the sobering message I was given back in time, twenty years ago. When I was done, an astounded Hans turned deathly pale, dropped his jaw in utter dread, and immediately charged out into another office close by, where I heard him shout, "Get Madam President on my secure line, now—*right frigging now!*"

ABOUT THE AUTHOR

George Baffour is a mixed-race German-Ghanaian with some Danish ancestry and is the grandson of the late, great Dr. Robert Patrick Baffour, OBE, OV—a celebrated Ghanaian academic and scientific inventor.

George Baffour holds an MBA (Distinction) from Hult International Business School (Dubai campus) and has previous BSc (Oceanography & Fisheries) and MPhil (Fisheries Science) degrees from the University of Ghana. He is a business professional with experience in the science, media and marketing industries. His career has spanned varied roles in a diverse range of entities—from Water Research Institute (WRI) of Council for Scientific and Industrial Research (CSIR, Ghana) to the American Fortune 500 company, 3M.

George is also an actor/musician—under the stage name *SoulKnight-Jazz*—and his acting credits include several TV productions in Ghana and Nigeria, notably the popular *Adams Apples Movie Series* by renowned award-winning director, Shirley Frimpong-Manso.

George Baffour published his first science-fiction/fantasy novel—*Bubble Joe and his fantastic journeys to Zapokrepit in the Land of the Day and a Half*—in 2008. The novelette *From Japan With Love Beyond Time* marks his return to storytelling after a decade of other academic and professional pursuits.

Printed in Great Britain
by Amazon